A Pinky Is a Baby Mouse

AND OTHER BABY ANIMAL NAMES

Pam Muñoz Ryan

illustrated by Diane deGroat

Hyperion Books for Children
New York

HYPERION BOOKS FOR CHILDREN

Printed in the United States of America.

First published in 1997 by Hyperion Books for Children.
    3 5 7 9 10 8 6 4 2

The artwork for each picture is prepared using watercolor.
This book is set in 15-point Stempel Schneidler.
Designed by Lara S. Demberg.

Library of Congress Cataloging-in-Publication Data

Ryan, Pam Muñoz.
    A pinky is a baby mouse, and other baby animal names / Pam
Muñoz Ryan ; illustrated by Diane deGroat— 1st ed.
    p. cm.
    Summary: Rhyming text explains the different names by which
various baby animals are known.
ISBN 0-7868-0240-5 (trade)—ISBN 0-7868-2190-6 (lib. bdg.)
1. Zoology—Nomenclature (Popular)—Juvenile literature.
2. Animals—Infancy—Juvenile literature. [1. Animals—Infancy.
2. Vocabulary.] I. deGroat, Diane, ill. II. Title.
QL355.R93   1997
591'.3'9014—dc20   95-25396

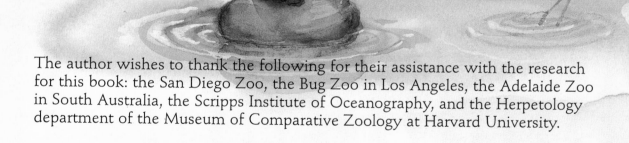

The author wishes to thank the following for their assistance with the research
for this book: the San Diego Zoo, the Bug Zoo in Los Angeles, the Adelaide Zoo
in South Australia, the Scripps Institute of Oceanography, and the Herpetology
department of the Museum of Comparative Zoology at Harvard University.

To Marcy, my first fledgling to leave the nest
—P. M. R.

Baby pigs are piglets
wallowing in the pen.

Kids are baby goats
ramming now and then.

Baby pigeons are squabs
perched near the windowpane.

I am a baby mouse.
Tell me, what's my name?

Cozy, rosy mouse
snuggling in the loft,
you are called a pinky
because you're pink and soft!

Baby trout are fingerlings
swimming in a school.

Polliwogs are baby frogs
growing in a pool.

Baby cranes are cranelings
pecking grass and grain.

I am a baby swan.
Tell me, what's my name?

Fluffy, scruffy swan
please do not forget,
you're not an 'ugly duckling.'
You're a beautiful cygnet!

Baby porcupines are kittens
chewing buds and bark.

Owlets are baby owls
blinking in the dark.

Glowworms are baby fireflies
but they don't have a flame!

I am a baby bat.
Tell me, what's my name?

Fuzzy, flying mammal
until you are grown-up,
you have a special name.
You are called a pup!

Baby jellyfish are ephyras
swimming with the tide.

Baby eels are elvers
finding a place to hide.

Baby seals are beach weaners
playing a slippery game.

I am a baby mackerel.
Tell me, what's my name?

Tiny, shiny mackerel
you're just a little tyke,
and until you grow much bigger
you are called a spike!

Baby giraffes are calves
browsing next to mother.

Baby hawks are eyas
nesting with each other.

Cubs are baby lions
tugging father's mane.

I am a baby zebra.
Tell me, what's my name?

Hobbly, wobbly zebra
at the water hole,
just like a baby horse,
you are called a foal!

Baby spiders are spiderlings
hiding beneath the leaves.

Baby monkeys are infants
chattering in the trees.

Baby crocodiles are hatchlings
resting in the rain.

I am a baby boa constrictor.
Tell me, what's my name?

Emerald Tree
BOA

Wiggly, squiggly boa
you'll be a heavyweight,
but while you are a newborn
you're called a neonate!

Joeys are baby kangaroos
riding up and down.

Baby spiny anteaters are puggles
sniffing a termite mound.

Baby emus are chicks
running on the plain.

I am a baby platypus.
Tell me, what's my name?

Teeny, weeny platypus
there's news that's sad but true.
Until somebody thinks of one
there is no name for you!

Nature Babies . . .

aardvark / *young*
alligator / *hatchling*
ant / *antling*
ant lion / *doodlebug*
badger / *cub*
bat / *pup*
bear / *cub*
beaver / *kit*
bird / *chick, nestling, fledgling*
buffalo / *calf*
bug / *nymph*
cat / *kitten*
chicken / *chick*
cockroach / *nymph*
codfish / *codling, hake, sprat*
cougar / *cub*
cow / *calf*
crab / *zoea, megalops*

crane / *craneling*
crocodile / *hatchling*
deer / *fawn, yearling, knobber, brocket*
dobsonfly / *hellgrammite*
dog / *puppy*
dolphin / *calf*
donkey / *foal*
dove / *squab*
dragonfly / *naiad*
duck / *duckling, flapper*
eagle / *eaglet*
eel / *elver*
elephant / *calf*
elk / *fawn, calf*
falcon / *eyas*
firefly / *glowworm*

fish / *fry, alevin*
fox / *cub, pup*
frog / *polliwog, tadpole, froglet*
froghopper / *spittlebug*
giraffe / *calf*
goat / *kid*
goose / *gosling, flapper*
gorilla / *infant*
grasshopper / *nymph*
grouse / *cheeper*
hare / *leveret*
hawk / *eyas*
hen / *pullet*
herring / *sprat*

hippopotamus / *calf*
horse / *foal*
jellyfish / *ephyra*
kangaroo / *joey*
koala / *joey*
lamprey / *ammocoetes*
lion / *whelp, cub*
louse / *nit*
mackerel / *tinker, spike*
midge / *glass worm*
monkey / *infant*
moose / *fawn, calf*
mouse / *pinky*
opossum / *young*
ostrich / *chick*
owl / *owlet*
oyster / *spat*

salmon / *parr, smolt, grilse*
seal / *beach weaner, pup*
shark / *pup*
sheep / *lamb, lambkin, lambling*
skunk / *young*
snail / *spat*
snake / *neonate (live birth), hatchling (egg)*
spider / *spiderling*
spiny anteater (echidna) / *puggle*
squirrel / *kitten*
swan / *cygnet, flapper*
tiger / *whelp, cub*
trout / *fingerling*
turkey / *poult*
turtle / *hatchling*
whale / *calf*
wolf / *whelp, pup*
yak / *calf*
zebra / *foal*

partridge / *squeaker*
penguin / *chick*
pheasant / *poult*
pig / *piglet, suckling, shoat, piggy*
pigeon / *squab, squeaker*
pilchard / *sardine*
platypus / *young*
porcupine / *kitten*
porpoise / *calf*
prairie dog / *pup*
quail / *cheeper*
rabbit / *bunny, kit*
raccoon / *kit*
rat / *pup*
rhinoceros / *calf*
rooster / *cockerel*